4

About the Book

Until his accident Superchief wasn't an especially unusual sort of pup.

Bouncy, flop-eared, big feet on legs so short they almost didn't reach the ground—yes.

Unusual—no, unless you consider it strange for a dog to make his home in an all-night CalaCo station with six humans, or unless Superchief's enthusiastic, wet-tongued, bouncing, tail-wagging greetings struck you as perhaps slightly out of the ordinary.

Then one day the accident happened, and it looked as though Superchief would never cavort or jump or greet again. But the Cala-crew's ingenuity turned disaster into a lifetime supply of dogfood, and before he knew it Superchief had become a bona fide celebrity.

William Corbin has created a wonderfully off-beat bunch of characters, including the most lovable and unpredictable pup you'll ever meet. All are brought hilariously and endearingly to life with illustrations by Charles Robinson.

THE PUP WITH THE
UP-AND-DOWN TAIL

by William Corbin Pseud.

William C. McGraw

Illustrated by Charles Robinson

Coward, McCann & Geoghegan, Inc.

New York

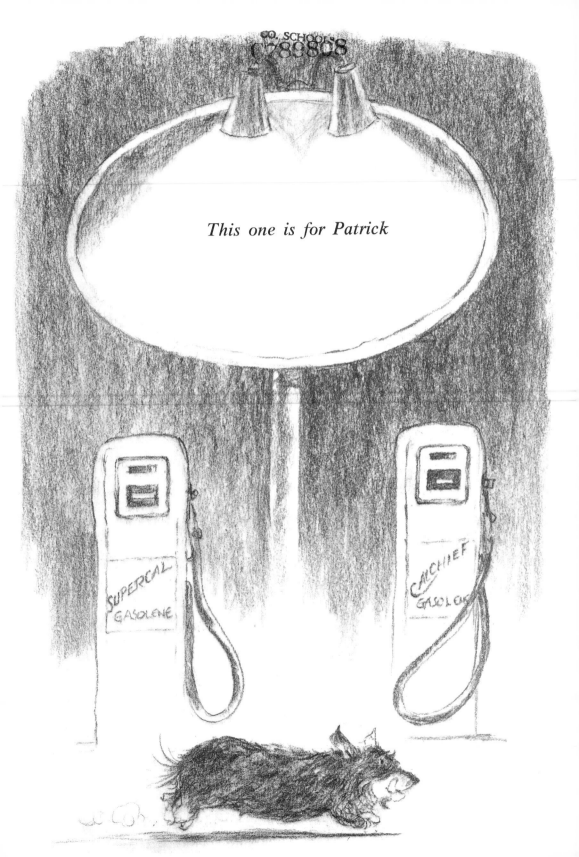

This one is for Patrick

1

Until his accident Superchief wasn't an especially unusual sort of pup.

Bouncy. Yes.

Flop-eared. Yes.

Curly-haired mostly-black-but-here-and-there-brownish. Yes.

Big feet on legs so short they almost didn't reach the ground. Yes.

Black eyes that burned with a fierce and friendly fire in their thicket of eyebrows and hair and whiskers. Yes.

Inclined to have narrow escapes and now and then a small accident. Yes.

Unusual—no. Just ordinary. At first, that is. But later—after the *bad* accident. . . .

Superchief lived at the CalaCo station at the corner of Maple and Main with Lew and Andy and JP (who couldn't *stand* "Jason Polonius") and Ol' Marvin and Maggie and Mr. MacInver. That is, Superchief lived there. The others only *worked* there. They kept going away to live lives unknown to him, in homes no telling where.

But they always came back. They came back at odd hours of the day and night (it was an all-night service station), and those were Superchief's most glorious times, because he was a natural-born greeter. A devout, hardworking, athletic, *noisy* natural-born greeter.

JP had a theory about this. (And JP ought to know, Ol' Marvin said, " 'Cause he's a young pup hisself.") The theory was that Superchief was firmly and unalterably convinced that anybody who went away would be gone forever.

"So when somebody *does* come back," JP was fond of explaining, "it's like he was back from the *dead*, and Super's just naturally got to sing out that hallelujah chorus!"

In any case, no astronaut back from the moon was ever more wildly welcomed than Superchief welcomed Ol' Marvin or JP or Lew or any of them when they came back for another shift at the gas pumps and lube racks. He would leap and whoop and bounce and yell and holler and cavort until whoever it was squatted down to where Superchief could get at him with his wet and loving tongue. And all the while his tail would be a fan-shaped blur behind him, so wildly was he wagging it.

It's true that each of them brought him something to eat, but on the rare occasions when they forgot or were too rushed or didn't have anything handy to bring, he greeted them in exactly the same way. Just for themselves.

He had no favorites, either, in spite of the fact that it was usually Andy and Lew who brought him the things he liked best of all to eat. Things like pepperoni pizza, slightly stale potato chips, the gristlier parts of not-very-well-cooked steaks, and leftover glops of frozen chocolate pies from the supermarket. Andy and Lew always had such delicacies on hand because they were bachelors, with no women-folk to see to it they had a Balanced Diet. (JP, at fifteen, wasn't old enough to be a bachelor.)

On the other hand, Maggie (whose name was really Mavis and who lived with Mr. MacInver because he was her father) was likely to bring Superchief sliced carrots and broccoli and rye bread crusts spread with yogurt because she thought he should have vitamins and other Nutritious Elements. Yet he welcomed her as joyously as any of the others. Maybe just a whisker's twitch more joyously because, next to him, she was the youngest of the crew. (She was eleven and he was ten. Years for her, months for him.)

Once, as a matter of fact, he welcomed her so joyously that it almost wrecked the place. That was when he saw her coming one morning and went charging around a corner and knocked over a stack of empty antifreeze cans (gallon size).

This caused so horrendous a clatter that a lady customer, intending to step on the brake when she got to a gas pump, got flustered and stepped on the accelerator instead, making scrap out of a display rack, two candy machines, and a trash barrel before she could pull herself together.

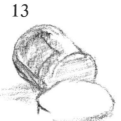

Another time he hurled himself at Ol' Marvin with such violence of affection that the old man lost his balance just enought to stagger against a fire extinguisher, causing it to leap from its bracket on the wall and spew its load of chemical foam all over the lube room. It took a week to clean up the mess and made Mr. MacInver wonder, in a menacing mutter, if they might need any fresh lion food out at the zoo.

After that (and a few other such incidents, some not so bad, some worse) Mr. MacInver, even though he didn't feed Superchief to the lions, always grumbled ominously whenever he brought him a marrow bone and made him go out back to chomp on it. Out where there were grass, and weeds with come-again fragrances, and lovely-stinky trash cans waiting to be hauled off.

Mr. MacInver made up for the grumbling, though, whenever somebody got in trouble on the freeway and a call for the tow truck came. He would hang up the phone and slowly tilt his gaze down to where Superchief was standing there *concentrating* up at him and vibrating like a small electric motor. Then, rumbling out some of the long words he was so fond of, Mr. MacInver would say, "Very well, you obnoxious omnivore," or something like that, "let's go!"

Out of that word batch, "go" was the only one Superchief understood, but he certainly understood *that*—all the way from "gee" to "oh"—and by the time Mr. MacInver had lumbered out to the big green-and-yellow tow truck and opened the door Superchief would have been all the way around it four times and under it twice, both ways.

Going in the tow truck with Mr. MacInver was the one thing in all the world he liked better than pepperoni pizza. High up on the seat of the truck amid the oily rags and the wrenches and things, he was King of Interstate Nine-Oh-Nine. Watch it, world—ol' Superchief's a-coming!

Lew and Andy. JP was still on the job, and Ol' Marvin had kept hanging around, getting whiter-whiskered by the minute, even though he was supposed to go home and get some sleep.

"We could use a watchdog around here!" said JP, who was inclined to be optimistic. "Might discourage robbers!"

"Hah!" snorted Mr. MacInver. "Any robber would have to be discouraged already to stick this place up, the way business has been. Anyway, he doesn't look much like a watchdog to me."

"You never know," said Lew, who was always Thinking Things Out. "Still waters run deep."

Mr. MacInver looked at Lew. "When I figure out what *that* is supposed to mean," he said, "I'll get in touch with you."

"He'd be a comfort to me," said Ol' Marvin. "Gets mighty lonesome at night sometimes. Give me somebody to talk to."

"Your language or his?" put in Andy, who considered himself, inaccurately, to be as witty as he was big and powerful.

18

"He'd be company for me, too," said JP hopefully. "I can get lonesome even with people around. Especially people like *Andy*."

Mr. MacInver was shaking his head. "Nice try, boys. But it won't do. First thing you know he'd get run over—little pup like that—and then how would you feel!? No—nothing to do but turn him over to the Humane Society."

Maggie, who hadn't *seemed* to be paying any attention, scooped up the subject of all this palaver from his nest in the drawer and folded her arms around him. "If you turn him over to the Humane Society," she said, "you'll have to turn *me* over, too. And I don't think that would be very humane."

There was a long and significant silence with all eyes fixed upon Mr. MacInver, who at last cast his own eyes upward and roared, "Ye gods and tribal fetishes! I am awash in a sea of sentimentalism!"

"What does *that* mean?" whispered JP to Maggie. Mr. MacInver's vocabulary tended to intimidate him.

"It means we keep Superchief," said Maggie matter-of-factly.

"Keep what?" said Lew.

"Keep who?" said JP.

"Superchief!" repeated Maggie, impatient with all this thickheadedness.

"Is that his name?" inquired Andy, whose head was as packed with muscle as the rest of him.

"Hey, that's right clever!" Ol' Marvin said, peering toward the red gas pumps, one labeled CALCHIEF and the other SUPERCAL. "Superchief! Now that's a real humdinger of a name!"

"Isn't anybody going to do any *work* around here?" said Mr. MacInver in a loud grumble.

3

That was the way Superchief at the age of seventy-one (days) got himself a name, a home, five masters, one mistress, and a career.

Before very long it got so the crew could hardly remember how MacInver's CalaCo had managed before Superchief showed up.

"Nothing like a dog," Andy said one day in April, "to give a filling station that lived-in feeling."

"With Superchief on the job," said Lew, along about June, "it's getting so that coming to work is more like coming home than going home is. If you see what I mean."

"If I saw what you mean, I'd be some kind of genius," said Andy.

"Put it this way," pursued Lew. "Going home seems more like going to work than going to work does. On account of Superchief. You follow me?"

"If I followed *you,* I'd end up in the funny farm," Andy said. But he really knew what Lew was getting at. Superchief did make the place seem like home—a great big neon-lighted home with open house day and night—and with only an occasional and insignificant accident.

"He's good for business," said Mr. MacInver, along about Fourth of July.

And that was true. It was true in the first place because of Superchief's rousing welcomes. After such a welcome nobody in Mr. MacInver's Calacrew (his very own word) could help starting off his day's work in the highest of spirits and the finest of fettles. This state of mind naturally rubbed off on the customers—even the grumpy ones—making them feel cheerful and welcome, too. So they came back oftener and spent more money, and Mr. MacInver began to think very seriously about giving everybody a raise.

In the second place, it made people feel good just to *look* at Superchief. As the months went by, he grew longer and broader and rounder— but he didn't grow any farther away from the ground. With longer legs he would have been a pretty big dog, but as it was (so Maggie said), he was a sort of *little* big dog.

He had to run three times the speed of other dogs in order to go as fast, so when he ran, he looked as if he were on wheels, like a roller skate. When he stood up, he seemed to be still sitting down. And vice versa. When he leaped, it looked like hiccups. And when people told him to lie down, they could never be sure he was doing it.

Unless, of course, he was lying on his back, which was what he always did when he was doing some really serious sleeping. Customers with urgent business elsewhere sometimes made themselves late just hanging around a few minutes longer to watch Superchief sleep.

With all four legs sticking up because they were too short to fold and his tail as rigid as a flagpole, he didn't look much like a dog and not much like anything else either.

"We ought to invent a brand-new species of animal," suggested JP (some time in August), "just for Superchief to be."

Lew, after a minute of thinking, said, "Sarawakian Slewfoot?"

"Antarctic Antelump?" contributed Maggie.

"The mini-minotaur from Minya-Konka," said Mr. MacInver, who could be counted on to top everybody because he knew so many words.

"*Is* there such a place," asked JP suspiciously, "as Minya what ever-you-said?"

"Scout's honor," said Mr. MacInver. "It's in China."

It was one of those times that come to all gas stations—when one batch of customers has driven away and the next one hasn't got there yet—and the crew had time to stand around a while watching Superchief sleep.

Smack in the middle of this interlude Superchief's tail began to wag—slowly at first, like a tree blowing in the wind. (A *stiff* tree). Then faster and faster until it looked like a whole collection of tails competing for the only dog around.

Asleep or awake, Superchief was one of the truly great tail waggers of the canine world. He wagged at sinner and saint alike. At friend or foe. At those with pepperoni to share and those with none. At rich man, poor man, beggarman, thief, and everybody else.

Looking down at him now, JP said, a little wistfully, "Wish I could trade dreams with him. Mine are so yucky."

Maggie sighed. "He's so funny," she said. "And so perfect. I hope nothing bad ever happens to him."

4

Just one week later, something bad did happen—Superchief's accident.

As with most accidents, it happened in a flash with no warning at all, and once it was done there could be no changing of it ever. Furthermore, this accident, unlike all the little ones that had gone before, wasn't even Superchief's fault—or anyway not altogether.

He had learned, in spite of those occasional lapses, that a filling station can be a dangerous place and that it was often a good idea to stay clear out of harm's way. For this purpose his favorite refuge was underneath the bottom shelf of the big rack of used tires that stood along one wall outside the lube room. There in good weather he could lie well protected, taking dognaps now and then but keeping one eye open in case somebody might show up who needed greeting.

30

He was doing the napping part of it the morning of the accident.

It was a balmy morning in early September. A gentle breeze was carrying mouth-watery fragrances across the highway from Lila's Anytime Eats. They were reaching Superchief in the middle of a dream, where they smelled even better, and his nose was twitching in appreciation. That was the moment when JP climbed up on the rack to get a tire from the top shelf.

A short stepladder stood nearby, but JP, who was sometimes as careless as Superchief, couldn't be bothered with that. He merely leaned a tire against the rack and stood on top of the tire, a feat which required no small balancing skill, particularly when a person was engaged in sliding another heavy tire out from between some others on the shelf above his head.

Because of this maneuver, the rack gave a shake and a jiggle, and Superchief woke up. Like anybody abruptly awakened, he was a bit confused for a moment and could thus be

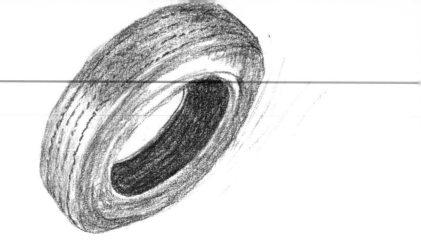

pardoned for leaping to the conclusion that he was about to miss a chance to greet somebody.

Accordingly he scrambled to his feet, charged out from under the rack, and ran smack into the leaning tire. The impact twisted it out from under JP's feet, and JP, grabbing wildly for a handhold on the shelf above him, let go of the tire he was holding, and it dropped—ker-FLUMP—whacking poor befuddled Superchief across the haunches like a giant's fist and knocking him spraddle-flat.

He lay quite still while the tire bounced twice and flopped down beside him. JP, feeling all hot and cold and horrible, let go of his hold and flopped down, too. He was about to scoop the little big dog up off the pavement when Superchief scrambled to his feet, staggered a bit, and shook himself all over.

JP scooped him up anyway and babbled apologies like crazy. Superchief let him know there were no hard feelings, but all the same JP felt awful—especially because Superchief hadn't let out so much as a single yip, though it must have hurt him something fierce.

That was nothing, though, to how terrible JP felt next morning when he came to work and heard Andy saying to Ol' Marvin, "Gosh-all-Friday—what's wrong with Superchief?"

What was wrong with Superchief was that his rear end wasn't working properly. When he spotted JP, he went straight into his welcoming routine. He whooped and yelled and hollered, and he *tried* to leap and bounce and cavort; but his hind legs kept collapsing under him. It was a

pitiful sort of welcome, and JP felt as if he'd swallowed a huge chunk of ice with jagged edges.

He felt even worse later on when he had to tell the whole story to Mr. MacInver and Maggie. They immediately dropped everything and took Superchief off to Doc Finsterwald. They took him in the tow truck. "For the sake of his morale," said Maggie in a voice so gently sad it made JP wish he could go off in a corner and sort of quietly bleed to death.

They were gone the better part of forever, and when they came back at last, there was a terrible shock for everyone.

The whole crew had gathered—including Lew, whose day off it was, and Ol' Marvin, who wasn't due on the job for hours. When there weren't any

cars to service, they all stood around not looking at one another and not saying anything unless they absolutely had to.

And at last when Maggie came, with her upper lip as stiff as steel, and Mr. MacInver carried Superchief in and laid him carefully down in his basket behind the desk, each of them made whatever odd, distressful little noise came natural.

Superchief was wearing a cast from just behind his front legs all the way to the base of his tail, and his shiny-black eyes peered out of their bristly thicket, hurt and fearful and bewildered.

Mr. MacInver did his best to explain what Doc Finsterwald had told him: Long, low dogs like Superchief often had back troubles which could be brought on by one mishap or another. (Out of compassion for JP he didn't mention falling tires.) "The wiring gets out of whack, you might say. A kind of short circuit, so the legs don't get the message from the brain. In other words"— and here Mr. MacInver gave a helpless kind of shrug "in other words—paralysis."

"But he'll get over it!" said JP, nearly yelling. *"Won't* he!"

Mr. MacInver gave him a long and somber look. Then he sighed and said, "We hope so, JP. Lord knows we hope so! The cast is to keep him from bending his back much. Then after two, three weeks Doc will take if off and we'll see—"

Maggie interrupted, speaking very firmly in order to be able to speak at all. "The answer, JP, is yes, he'll get over it. But we've got to *help* him!" She looked around and up in a sort of glare at all those man-type creatures of various shapes and sizes, and they all shifted their feet and their eyes and looked about as helpless as Superchief in his white cocoon.

Andy, who looked the most helpless of all because of his size and strength, scowled ferociously, which was what he always did when deep thought was called for, and said, "Sure, Maggie—we got to help! Only—only—"

But Maggie wasn't listening because her mental gears were whirring around so fast. "We've got to do something for his morale!" she

38

said. "We can't let him just *lie* there. We've got to fix it so he can get around—and we've got to do it quick—like maybe *tomorrow!*"

"But Maggie-child!" pleaded Mr. MacInver, rumpling his hair distractedly with both hands. "You know what Doc—"

Maggie wasn't listening to him either because she had turned as stiff as Superchief's tail and was staring through the doorway into the lube room. She was staring at the little rack with rollers on it the men used when they lay on their backs to work on the undersides of cars.

Then she whirled around, her face glowing. "Lew!" Her voice was so high with excitement that everybody jumped. "Lew—you're the best at making things. What you've got to do is make a little scooter thing—you know, with wheels or rollers—that will fasten onto Superchief's cast. . . ."

5

Right there was the exact moment in the life of Superchief when he stopped being an ordinary, bouncy, flop-eared, curly-haired, fiendish-eyed, whiskery pup and started turning into a bona fide Celebrity.

The scooter thing looked like a success from the very start, Lew being so clever and all; but using it was up to Superchief, and nobody knew how *that* would turn out.

It was a little platform shaped to fit the underside of the cast, to which it could be fastened with strong elastic straps. At its rear end it was high enough so that Superchief's feet wouldn't touch the ground. Substituting for feet was a set of hard-rubber casters that would swivel in any direction. The idea was that when he decided to go somewhere with his front legs, which nothing was wrong with, the rest of him would come right along.

There was quite an audience on hand for Superchief's maiden voyage. It included the whole Cala-crew, plus four or five customers who figured they might as well see what was going on since they weren't getting any service anyway.

Lew set Superchief gently down on the contraption and fastened the straps. Then Maggie, down on her knees in front of the candy-bar machine, made the chirruppy sound he liked so well. He gave a twitch with his ears, to show her he had got the message but that there was nothing he could do about it. But Maggie went on. "Now, Super, you can do it. You're on wheels now—so *come*."

Well, when she talked like that, there was nothing for a little big dog to do but try. So he tried—and the contraption rolled backward about four inches. Everybody made small groaning sounds. Everybody except Maggie, that is. She said, "Now will you just quit clowning and come here to me!"

Superchief peered up and around at all those faces that looked so eager and hopeful and apprehensive, and he tried to wag his tail apologetically, forgetting that it simply wouldn't wag. The last face he looked at belonged to Mr. MacInver, who shrugged with resignation. "Might as well do it, Super," he advised. "She's got her mind made up."

This was so obviously true that Superchief tried again. And again the scooter thing rolled backward. This time the general groan was a little more distressed, and a lady customer said, "Ohhh, the poor little thing!"

Superchief twitched his ears twice as hard because he couldn't wag his tail—and a tiny little whine came out of him, on a note so high it seemed to be coming from somewhere up around Andy's head.

Tears came all-unasked-for into Maggie's eyes as she knelt on the unfriendly pavement, but she pressed her lips together and made her jaw be as firm as a jaw that small could ever be and said,

43

"Superchief MacInver, you just stop feeling sorry for yourself and come . . . right . . . here . . . to . . . me!" She had actually forgotten there was anybody there but her and Superchief. She blinked her eyes hard so that she could see straight into his and made the chirruppy sound once more.

Everybody held his breath, and Superchief, wildly rolling his eyes so that they showed a gleaming white around the edges, hunched his shoulders and with a prodigious effort, took what was obviously meant to be a Great Leap Forward.

It was neither great nor a leap; but it was definitely forward, and the audience let out a cheer. All except Maggie, who made the chirruppy sound again, and this time Superchief managed something very much like a trot, and in a moment she had her arms around him and her face down where he could get at it with his wet and loving tongue. JP was whacking Lew on the

back and whooping, "It works—it works! You did it!"

Lew, in his low and modest tone, was saying, "I thought up a name for it. I call it the Pup-mobile."

Because of all the noise and confusion and because of the low and modest tone, Lew's remark went unheard by all but one pair of ears. This pair belonged to one of the customers, a medium-sized man with a medium-sized mustache, who went quick as a flash to his car and got out a camera that looked as if it had been to a lot of places. "Young lady," he said to Maggie, "may I take a picture or two of you and your dog?"

"*Our* dog," Maggie corrected him. "The whole Cala-crew's."

The stranger appeared to be lost in wonder and admiration. "Cala-crew," he muttered to himself. "Pupmobile. Superchief. Oh, I must have been living right!"

Maggie looked at him severely. "Talking to yourself is a bad sign," she said.

He looked startled, then grinned. "All newsmen are nuts," he said. "I work for the Associated Press. Now if you'll just get down over there—the way you were—and give ol' Super-chief the word...."

6

Within a week there could hardly have been a soul in the entire United States of America who hadn't heard about Superchief and his Pup-mobile and Maggie MacInver. The Associated Press man had taken a lot of photographs, and the one he chose to send out all over the country on wirephoto was the kind—as he said to Mr. MacInver—that "turns the flinty hearts of editors to cottage cheese."

Though he wasn't about to admit it, it turned Mr. MacInver's heart to cottage cheese too, the moment he saw it staring at him next morning from the front page of the big-city paper, and the first chance he got he sneaked off and bought a dozen extra copies.

The photograph showed Superchief, both ears flapping like mad as he trundled along on the Pupmobile toward Maggie, whose arms were stretched eagerly and whose face was lighted up with a glow that was welcoming and tender. She looked (Ol' Marvin said) "as purty as the first Easter egg in the basket."

After the picture came out in the paper, things began to get confusing in a hurry. The next day a set of men with television cameras showed up and did all sorts of things. They even fast-talked Lew into performing with Superchief in front of a gas pump, pretending to be filling the Pupmobile with SuperCal.

Next thing anybody knew, the place was swarming with CalaCo men, and they had cameras, too. Next came the Fido-Fodder dog food people, and *they* photographed everything in sight (first giving Mr. MacInver a very large check for the privilege of doing it). They also promised to send Superchief a lifetime supply of Fido-Fodder. Whether he wanted it or not.

Mr. MacInver promptly divided the money among the crew members, remarking, as he did so, that he for one was fed up to *here* with publicity. "Superchief," he said with a commanding air, "from now on any man who shows up with a camera—you bite him! Set upon him savagely! Understand?"

Superchief twitched his ears and rolled his eyes and panted to show that he was more than ready for whatever he was supposed to be ready for.

JP looked down at him sadly and then at the check in his hand. "Being a man of means is great," he said, "but I'd give my whole share just to see that silly tail wag again."

All the men sighed and nodded gloomy agreement. But not Maggie, who said, "Well, I don't know about you, but *I'm* going to see him wag it anyway!"

51

7

As she had a way of doing, Maggie turned out to be right—though not at all in the way she had expected.

Near the end of the third week after Superchief's accident Doc Finsterwald took off the cast, which by this time looked grubby and smelled grubbier. Then he gave Superchief three shots in the seat of the pants and said, "He won't be chasing any tigers yet awhile—and maybe he never will, but—but all we can do is wait and see."

And wait they did—the whole Cala-crew. All that morning they waited, and all that afternoon, and Superchief just lay in his basket looking sorrowful and bewildered because he didn't have a scooter any more and didn't know how to do without one.

Six o'clock came, then seven o'clock, then eight. It was a Saturday night, and everybody was very busy at the pumps, for which they were grateful because it kept them from thinking so hard about the plight of the poor little big dog.

At three and one-half minutes after eight a customer starting through the door was nearly knocked slaunchwise as JP came exploding out, yelling at the top of his voice, "He's scratching! He's *scratching!* He's got an itch and he's SCRATCHING!"

While all the customers sat in their cars wondering what manner of madness was afoot, the Cala-crew clustered around Superchief's basket like a clutch of hens around a hatching egg and exuberantly watched Superchief scratch. He wasn't very good at it at first because his foot, all out of practice, had trouble finding its way to the itch. But it didn't matter because if he missed one itch, there was another right next to it. (Because he had been inside the cast so long.)

From that moment he began to recuperate. He spent the night alternately scratching, napping, and learning to walk again without the aid of the Pupmobile. The next day Maggie gave him a bath. It was only the second bath he had had in his entire life and it was a Harrowing Experience. It also led to a startling discovery.

She gave him his bath in the tank in which tire tubes were tested. First she rubbed him all over with soothing anti-itch goo that smelled heavenly to her and hideous to him, and then she lathered him with shampoo, rinsed him in two changes of water, and rubbed him vigorously enough with towels to make him wish he were back in his nice stinky cast again. Then at last she put him down and sat back on her heels and told him in her most chirruppy tone that he was the handsomest, curliest, bristliest, shiniest, cleanest, *fragrantest* little big dog in the *en*-tire animal kingdom.

Well, in the face of all that praise and approbation, what could a little big dog do but wag his tail?

Wag his tail?

But he hadn't wagged his tail in weeks!

Maggie didn't even notice it right off, because she was looking deep into his black and fiendish eyes. But Andy, who was hurrying by on his way to get a can of transmission fluid, stopped in mid-stride and let out a startled "Hey!"

Then Maggie noticed. Superchief's tail was going faster—faster—faster. . . . But it wasn't going from side to side as it had always gone before. It was. . . .

Before she could convince herself it was really so, Andy, sounding stunned, put it into words: "Good gosh-all-Friday, Maggie—That pup's got an up-and-down tail!"

And so he had.
At first everybody thought it was some kind of
temporary phenomenon that would go away once

Superchief remembered how a tail really should be wagged. But a day passed, and a night, and another day—and still he went on wagging it up and down, up and down. Never from side to side like all other dogs in the *en*-tire animal kingdom.

"Wait till I tell Doc Finsterwald!" Mr. MacInver said. "This pup will make veterinary history!"

Maggie thought about that awhile. Then she shook her head. "'I think he's made quite enough history already."

After a moment Lew nodded. "Maybe you've got something there, Maggie."

"Yeah!" said Andy.

"Durn tootin'!" put in Ol' Marvin. "First thing we'd have a whole hive of them vettinarians a-swarmin' all around till the poor little dog wouldn't have no peace."

They sat around for a minute nodding at one another.

"They'd want to *X*-ray him!" said Andy. He made it sound like some horrible form of torture.

"And *operate* on him!" contributed JP.

59

"Or else operate on a lot of *other* dogs," said Lew, who had been thinking harder than anybody, "in order to start a fad for dogs with up-and-down tails."

"Durned if they wouldn't!" Ol' Marvin said. "For all them bitty narrow trailer houses!"

"So Superchief would be the father of a whole new breed of dog," pursued JP, getting carried away, "and they'd offer us millions of dollars for him and—"

"Well, we wouldn't sell him!" said Maggie fiercely.

"So they'd *steal* him!" whooped JP.

"Andbody tries that," rumbled Andy, murderously rippling his muscles, "I'll break him in pieces! I'll tear his arm off and—"

Suddenly Mr. MacInver cleared his throat with a sound like the ripping of sheets and said, "Gentlemen! If I promise to perpetuate the canine status quo on these premises, *could* you bring yourselves to knock off the phantasmagoria and GO WAIT ON THE CUSTOMERS?"

First chance he got when the dust had settled, JP sidled up to Maggie and muttered, "What for gosh sakes did all *that* mean?"

Smiling a slightly smug but altogether triumphant smile, Maggie gave Superchief a pat on his bristly brow and answered, "It means he doesn't have to get any more famous than he's already got." She stopped smiling and frowned a little instead, because she was concentrating. "It means it doesn't really matter," she went on, "whether or not we've got the world's only pup with an up-and-down tail; all that matters really is we've got Superchief, just for himself. And we'll go on having him for a long, long time."

62

And that—because Maggie had a way of being right about most things—was exactly how it all turned out.

About the Author

William Corbin needs little introduction. He is the author of many fine books for young people. Among them are *Smoke, Golden Mare,* both winners of the Pacific Northwest Library Association Young Readers Choice Award, *High Road Home,* awarded the Child Study Association honor award in 1955, *The Everywhere Cat* and *The Day Willie Wasn't,* two picture books for the very young, and most recently, *The Prettiest Gargoyle.*

Mr. Corbin and his wife, Eloise Jarvis McGraw, live in a house atop Indian Mountain in Lake Oswego, Oregon, from which they have a spectacular view of Mount Hood.

About the Artist

Charles Robinson is a graduate of Milton Academy, Harvard College, and the University of Virginia Law School. A member of the New Jersey Bar, he gave up practicing law in 1968 to devote full time to the illustration of children's books, and has been remarkably successful. He wrote and illustrated *Yuri and the Mooneygoats,* and has illustrated thirty-five other books for young readers. In 1971 he won the Society of Illustrators' Gold Medal.

Charles Robinson, his wife Cynthia, and their three children live in New Vernon, New Jersey.